Vol. 6: Pirates' End?

Adapted from the novel by ROBERT LOUIS STEVENSON

THE STORY SO FAR:

Jim Hawkins relates how seaman *Billy Bones* died at his family's "Admiral Benbow" inn on the English coast. A treasure map in his sea-chest proved he had been in the crew of the late pirate *Captain Flint*. With *Dr. Livesey*, *Squire Trelawney*, and *Captain Smollett*, Jim sailed in search of gold on the schooner Hispaniola.

But one-legged **Long John Silver** and others of Flint's old crew sailed with them and seized the ship. The treasure-hunters and their servants held out on stockade on the isle, while Jim encountered wild-looking **Ben Gunn**, another one-time Flint crewman.

Later, Jim managed to liberate the Hispaniola. But, returning to the stockade, he found it in the pirates' hands and he was captured. The mutineers were ready to rebel against Silver, but, map in hand and his parrot "Captain Flint" on his shoulder, he led them off to find the buried treasure. Yet, there were ld omens. On a hilltop they found a skeleton in seaman's garb... then a voice from nowhere began singing, "Fifteen men on the dead man's chest...." And one of the pirates swore it sang with the voice of the dead Captain Flint....

Writer	Penciler	Inker	Colorist
Roy Thomas	Mario Gully	Pat Davidson	SotoColor's A. Crossley

Letterer	Cover	Production	Assistant Editor
Virtual Calligraphy's Joe Caramagna	Greg Hildebrandt	Irene Lee	Lauren Sankovitch

Associate Editor	Editor	Editor in Chief	Publisher
Nicole Boose	Ralph Macchio	Joe Quesada	Dan Buckley

VISIT US AT
www.abdopublishing.com

Reinforced library bound edition published in 2009 by Spotlight, a division of the ABDO Group, 8000 West 78th Street, Edina, Minnesota 55439. Spotlight produces high-quality reinforced library bound editions for schools and libraries. Published by agreement with Marvel Characters, Inc.

Library of Congress Cataloging-in-Publication Data

Thomas, Roy, 1940-
  Treasure Island / adapted from the novel by Robert Louis Stevenson ; Roy Thomas, writer ; Mario Gully, penciler ; Pat Davidson, inker ; SotoColor's A. Crossley, colorist ; VC's Joe Caramagna, letterer. -- Reinforced library bound ed.
      v. cm.
   "Marvel."
   Contents: v. 1. Treasure Island -- v. 2. Treasure Island part 2 -- v. 3. Mutiny on the Hispaniola -- v. 4. Embassy--and attack -- v. 5. In the enemy's camp -- v. 6. Pirates' end?
   ISBN 9781599616018 (v. 1) -- ISBN 9781599616025 (v. 2) -- ISBN 9781599616032 (v. 3) -- ISBN 9781599616049 (v. 4) -- ISBN 9781599616056 (v. 5) -- ISBN 9781599616063 (v. 6)
   Summary: Retells, in comic book format, Robert Louis Stevenson's tale of an innkeeper's son who finds a treasure map that leads him to a pirate's fortune.
   [1. Stevenson, Robert Louis, 1850-1894. --Adaptations. 2. Graphic novels. 3. Buried treasure--Fiction. 4.Pirates--Fiction. 5. Adventure and adventurers--Fiction. 6. Caribbean Area--History--18th century--Fiction.] I. Stevenson, Robert Louis, 1850-1894. II. Gully, Mario. III. Davidson, Pat, 1965- IV. Crossley, Andrew.
V. Caramagna, Joe. VI. Title.
PZ7.7.T518 Tre 2009
[Fic]--dc22   2008035322

All Spotlight books have reinforced library bindings and
are manufactured in the United States of America.

They was Flint's last words--his last words above board!

P-please forgive me my sins, Lord!

I was well brought up, before I came to sea and fell among bad companions!

That fixes it! *Let's go!*

Nobody in this here island ever heard of Darby--not one of us but what's here.

But--shipmates, I never was feared of Flint in his life, and, by the powers, I'll face him dead.

There's 700,000 pound not a quarter mile from here. When did ever a gentleman o' fortune shown his stern to that mud dollars, for a boozy old seaman with a blue mug--and him *dead,* too!

Pieces of eight--pieces of eight--⁒sqwawkk⁒

Belay there, John! Don't you cross a spirit!

Spirit? Well, maybe...

But there was an *echo.*

Now, no man ever seen a spirit with a shadow--so what's he doing with an echo to him, I should like to know?

Come to think on it, it was like Flint's voice--but it was liker somebody *else's* voice.

It was liker to--to--

By the powers-- **BEN GUNN!**

The first of the tall trees was reached...

Check the bearing.

It's the wrong one.

So with the second...

Not this'un, neither.

The third rose nearly two hundred feet in the air...

It's this one, right enough, by the bearing!

It's so visible far out to sea, it's like to have been entered as a sailing mark upon the chart.

And the gold lies buried somewhere beneath its great shadow!

Move, blast ye, boy!

Silver plucked furiously at the line that held me to him...

And I read his thoughts like print.

If he found the treasure, he hoped to cut every honest throat about the island and sail away, laden with crimes and riches.

Shaken as I was with these alarms, now and again I stumbled...

Hnnnhh

Up with you, boy--or I'll stop bein' so gentle!

"Lord, th-though I walk through the...the valley"... blast my eyes..."of the shadow of d-death..."

Dick's fever kept rising.

To crown all, I was haunted by the thought of the tragedy that had once been acted on that plateau...

...when Captain Flint, that ungodly buccaneer, had, with his own hand, cut down his six accomplices.

We were now at the margin of the thicket...

Huzzah, mates, all together!

Don't you dare start without me, you bilge rats!

Come on, you!

Jim...take this double-barreled pistol, and stand by for trouble.

The buccaneers, with oaths and cries, leaped one after another into the pit and dug with their fingers.

At the same time, Silver began moving quietly northward, and in a few steps had put the hollow between us two and the other five.

I found something!

A two-guinea piece!

Two guineas!

That's your 700,000 pounds, is it, Silver?

You bungled it, you wooden-headed lubber!

Dig away, boys.

You'll find some pig-nuts, I shouldn't wonder.

Pig-nuts! Mates, do you hear that?

I tell you now, that man there knew it all along.

Look in the face of him, and you'll see it wrote there!

The pirates began to scramble out of the excavation.

But one thing I observed which looked well for us...

They had all got out upon the opposite side from Silver.

Standing for cap'n, are you?

You're a pushing lad, to be sure.

Mates, there's two of them alone there.

The old cripple that brought us all here--and that cub I mean to have the heart of.

Now, mates--

He was raising his arm and his voice, and plainly meant to lead a charge...

But, just then, from the thicket--

KRAK KRAK KRAK

I reckon I settled you.

Forward, Gray!

Double-quick, Mr. Gunn!

We must head 'em off the boats.

And we set off at a great pace, sometimes plunging through the bushes to our chest.

I'll tell you, but Silver was anxious to keep up with us.

When we reached the brow of the slope...

Doctor-- see there!

No hurry!

This was Flint's treasure that we had come so far to seek...

...and that had cost already the lives of seventeen men from the Hispaniola.

How many had it cost in the amassing?

What good ships scuttled on the deep-- what brave men walking the plank--what shame and lies and cruelty-- no man alive could tell.

Yet there were three upon that island who had taken his share in these crimes.

You're a good boy in your line, Jim...but I don't think you and me'll go to sea again.

You're too much of the born favorite for me.

What a supper I had of it that night, with all my friends around me.

Never, I am sure, were people gayer or happier.

And there was Silver, eating heartily--the same bland, polite, obsequious seaman of the voyage out.

The next morning we fell early to work...

...with a single sentry on guard against the three pirates still at liberty.

Gray and Ben Gunn came and went with the boat...

...while the rest, during their absence, piled treasure on the beach.

As I was not much use at carrying, I was kept busy all day in the cave...

...packing the minted money into bread-bags.

It was a strange collection, like Billy Bones's hoard for the diversity of coinage.

The pictures of all the kings of Europe for the last hundred years...Oriental pieces...nearly every variety of money in the world.

For three days this work went on...with no sign of the surviving mutineers.

On the third night, the Doctor and I were strolling on the shoulder of the hill...

...when the wind brought us a snatch of sound between shrieking and singing.

♫...but one **man of her crew** alive...♫

Heaven forgive them...'tis the mutineers!

All drunk, sir.

Drunk or raving.

Right you were, sir...and precious little odds which, to you and me.

My feelings may surprise you, Master Silver.

But if I were sure they were raving-- as I am morally certain that one, at least, of them is down with fever--

--I would leave this camp and, at whatever risk to my own carcass, take them the assistance of my skill.

Ask your pardon, sir, but you would lose your life, and you may lay to that.

Those men down there, they couldn't keep their word--no, not supposing they wished to.

No. *You're* the man to keep your word...we know that.

That was the last news we had of the three pirates.

Only once, we heard a gunshot a great way off, and supposed them to be hunting.

We held a council, and it was decided we must desert them on the island...

...to the huge glee of Ben Gunn, and with the strong approval of Gray.

We left a good stock of powder and shot, the bulk of the salted goat, a few medicines, and other necessaries...

...in the cave atop the two-pointed hill.

And at last, one fine morning, we weighed anchor and stood out of North Inlet...

...the same colors flying that the Captain had flown and fought under at the palisade.

But the three fellows must have been watching us closer than we thought...

For, as we sailed past the southern point, we saw them kneeling on a spit of sand, their arms raised in supplication.

WE CANNOT RISK ANOTHER MUTINY-- AND A GALLOWS AWAITS YOU AT HOME--

BUT WE LEFT STORES IN THE CAVE!

But they continued to call out, for God's sake, not to leave them to die in such a place...

When they saw that the ship still bore on her course...

She's drawing out of earshot!

RRRAARRR

KRAKK

After that, we kept under cover of the bulwarks until that spit of sand had almost melted out of sight with the growing distance.

And before noon, to my inexpressible joy, the highest rock of Treasure Island had sunk into the blue round of sea.

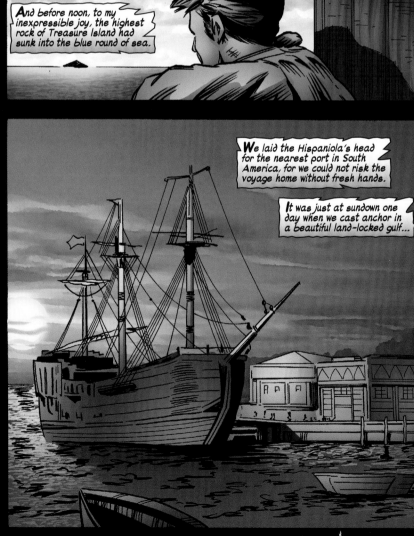

We laid the Hispaniola's head for the nearest port in South America, for we could not risk the voyage home without fresh hands.

It was just at sundown one day when we cast anchor in a beautiful land-locked gulf...

All of us had an ample share of the treasure, and used it wisely or foolishly, according to our natures.

Captain Smollett is now retired from the sea.

Gray saved his money, studied his profession, and is now mate and part owner of a fine full-rigged ship.

As for Ben Gunn, he got a thousand pounds, which he spent or lost in nineteen days, and was back begging on the twentieth.

He still lives, and is a notable singer in church on Sundays and saints' days.

Of Silver we heard no more...but I daresay he still lives in comfort with his wife and Captain Flint.

It is to be hoped, for his chances of comfort in another world are very small.